WHADAYAMEAN

For my mother and father who
would have liked to change the world

First published 1999
1 3 5 7 9 10 8 6 4 2

Copyright © 1999 John Burningham
John Burningham has asserted his right
under the Copyright, Designs and Patents Act, 1988,
to be identified as the author of this work

First published in the United Kingdom in 1999 by
Jonathan Cape Ltd.
20 Vauxhall Bridge Road, London SW1V 2SA

A CIP catalogue record of this book is
available from the British Library

ISBN 0 224 04753 1

Printed in Singapore by
Tien Wah Press (Pte), Ltd.

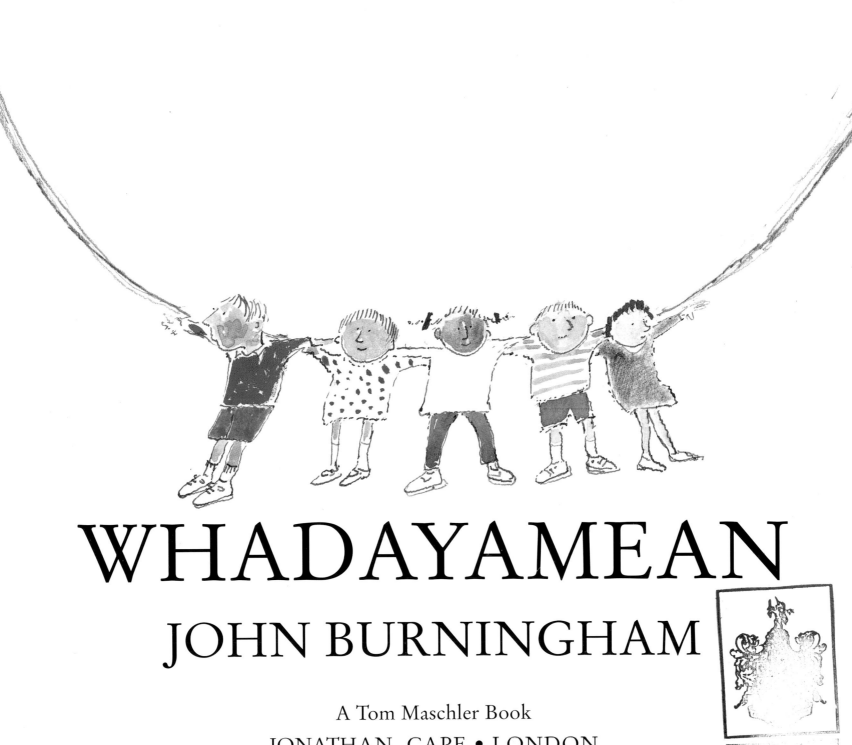

WHADAYAMEAN

JOHN BURNINGHAM

A Tom Maschler Book

JONATHAN CAPE • LONDON

It took millions of years to make planet Earth and God was very pleased when finally there was a paradise where animals and people could live with air to breathe and water to drink.

The stars that you see in the sky at night don't have any people or animals or plants because God couldn't make them work.

God was tired after making planet Earth and went to sleep for a very long time. Then one day God woke and decided to visit the planet that was still paradise. But not wanting to be seen, God caused a deep sleep to fall upon the people.

And while everybody slept, God started to look around the world. There were two children who were playing under a very large and old cedar tree who had not gone to sleep. And God came to them and said, 'Why are you not asleep like everyone else?'

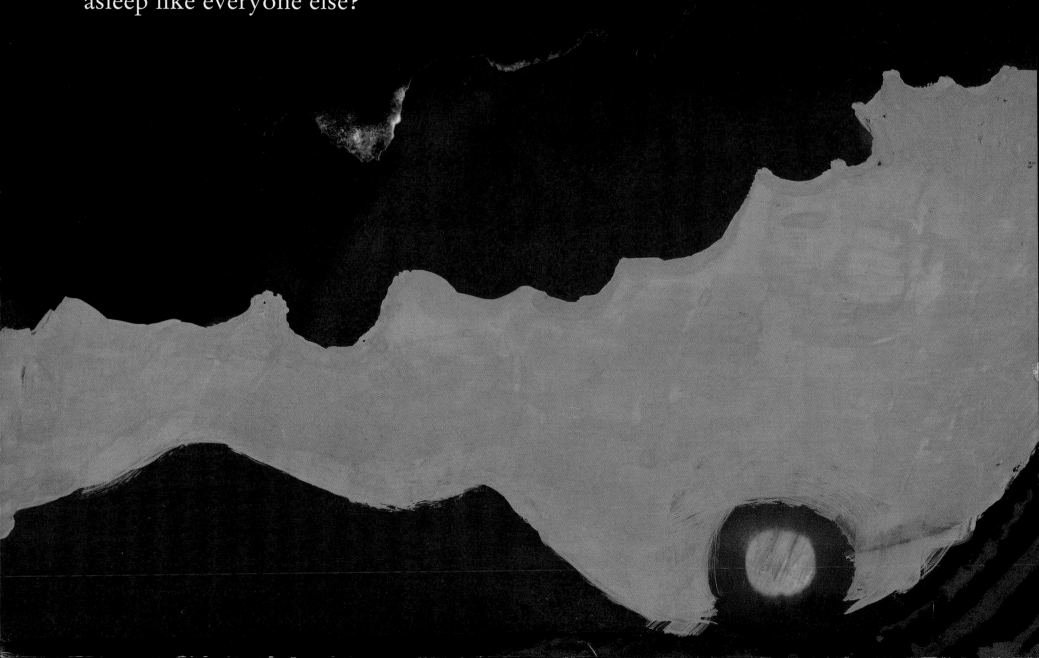

'We are not asleep,' said the children, 'because we are playing a game under the cedar tree.'
And God said, 'Since you are not asleep you must come with me and look at my world.'

And so the children set off with God to look at the world.
And God said, 'I do not like the things I see.'

'The waters of the sea which I made for the fishes and the birds are filthy and dirty.'

'The air which I made clean and fresh for you to breathe
has been filled with fumes which are foul and nasty.'

'The forests which are home to the plants, birds and animals are being chopped down and burned. Many living things have gone forever and I cannot make them again.

There seem to be an awful lot of you people. I made you the most clever of all creatures so you would look after the world.'

'And look at the ice which I made for the penguins and polar bears. It is melting now and getting very thin and parts of the world will soon be flooded.'

'There are many of you who do not have enough to eat and there are many who seem to have too much. You have spoiled my lovely world.'

'We're only little children.
We're not old enough to spoil your world.
What do you want us to do?'

They had stopped in a place which God liked and they had a
picnic. And the animals and birds came too for they had no
fear because God was there. And God said, 'You must go and
tell the grown-ups to change the way they are living.'

'Grown-ups won't listen to us,' said the little children.
'They will listen if you tell them that I told you to,' God said.
'I will come back again when the world is a better place.'

And so the little children set out to find the men with
the money who cut down the trees, dirtied the waters and
fouled the air.
'We must save the world,' the children told them. 'Stop
cutting the trees, dirtying the waters and fouling the air.'
'Whadayamean? Don't waste our time, you snotty little
kids. You can't tell us what not to do. Run away, we're busy.'

'But God said to tell you not to cut trees, dirty the waters
and foul the air.'
'Oh, if it was *God* who said we must not do this, then we
must stop,' said the men with the money.

The children went to see the people who said they spoke for
God and who were always quarrelling amongst themselves.
'We must save the world. You must stop quarrelling
amongst yourselves.'
'Whadayamean? You foolish little children that have
lost your way, you cannot tell us not to quarrel
amongst ourselves.'

'But God said to tell you,' answered the children.
'Oh if *God* said to tell us then we must all stop
quarrelling,' said the people who did speak for God.

Then the children went forth to see the men who had the guns and the bombs that hurt and that killed.
And the children said, 'We must save the world. You must throw away those horrid things that hurt and kill.'
'Whadayamean, you twitty children? You can't tell us what to do with our guns and bombs.'
'We *can* tell you,' said the children, 'because God said to tell you.'
'Oh, if God said so we must throw away the guns and bombs,' said the men in the uniforms.

Finally the children gathered together all the people who stood by and took no notice of what was happening to the world.
'We must save the world. Look at what is happening. You must change your ways.'
'Whadayamean you horrid little whining brats?' shouted the people. 'Who do you think you are, telling us what to do.'

'But it is God who said to tell you to change your ways to save the world.'

'Oh, if it is *God* who said we must change our ways, then we must change at once,' said the people who took no notice of what was happening around them.

And so it came to pass that the men with the money stopped cutting the trees, dirtying the waters and fouling the air.

And those who said they spoke for God stopped quarrelling amongst themselves.

And the men in the uniforms who had the guns
and the bombs that hurt and killed people threw
them away.

And the people who stood by and took no notice of what was happening to the world changed their ways.

And those who did not have enough to eat had
enough to eat.
And the world became a better world.

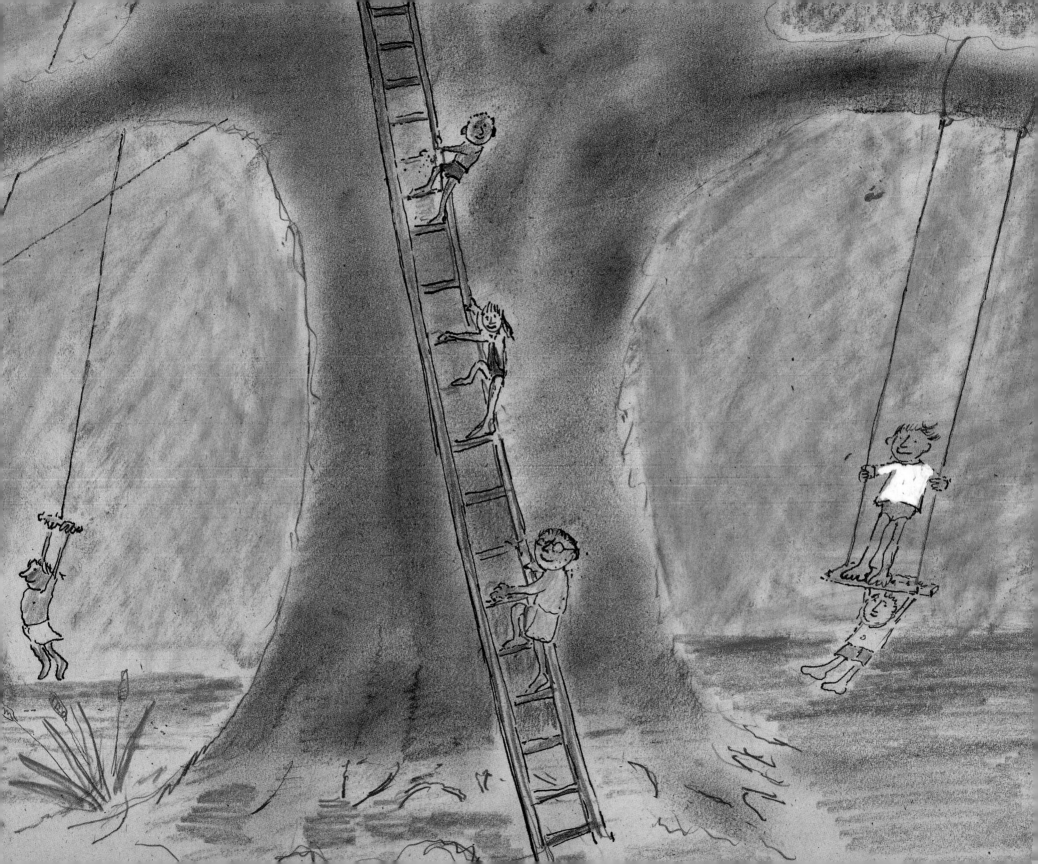

And time did pass. And God decided to visit the world
and returned to the cedar tree where the children had
been playing.
And God called to them and said, 'Show me my world.'